About the author

George Georgallis was born in Cyprus. He spent some of his childhood years at school in East London. As a foreign exchange student, he attended high school in Wisconsin, USA and university in London, where he qualified and practiced as a solicitor for over twenty-five years. Having returned to Cyprus, he shares his time between enjoying the cosmopolitan city of Limassol and his cherry orchard in the Troodos Mountains, visiting London on a frequent basis.

BILLIONAIRE AND THE DOLPHINS

GEORGE GEORGALLIS

BILLIONAIRE AND THE DOLPHINS

Vanguard Press

A CIP catalogue record for this title is
available from the British Library.

ISBN 978 1 78465 794 9

Vanguard Press is an imprint of
Pegasus Elliot MacKenzie Publishers Ltd.
www.pegasuspublishers.com

First Published in 2022

Vanguard Press
Sheraton House Castle Park
Cambridge England

Printed & Bound in Great Britain

CHAPTER ONE

The descent of the paparazzi to this small Greek island in the Cyclades resembled the tsunami that had, centuries before, destroyed the nearby civilization of Atlantis, albeit from different causes; the tsunami was caused by an earthquake, the descent of the myriad paparazzi by a birthday.

The earthquake happened about four thousand years ago. The birth of Edward Rayleigh-Miller, the only child of Charles Rayleigh-Miller and Lady Lucinda Rayleigh-Miller, happened sixty years ago today on the 31st day of July 2018.

Unlike the nearby islands of Mykonos and Santorini, the island, named Elios meaning *the sun*, despite its many natural attractions — long sandy beaches, clear blue waters — was not discovered by the jet setters until the twenty-first century and even then, only to a limited extent. Its preservation throughout the post-war and cold war periods was due to Charles and Lucinda, Edward's parents, who visited the island in the fifties, fell in love with it and with each other, and married at the local church on that their first visit. The date on their marriage certificate more or less coincided with the date of Edwards conception.

What had attracted the couple to the island initially was Lucinda's wish to spot and photograph the Elios blue orchid, a flower indigenous to the island. In fact, for the next years of their lives together Charles would, on the first day of each month, give his wife a blue orchid, a tradition which not only remained a family secret but which, on the death of his father, Edward carried on by personally delivering to his mother a blue orchid on the first day of each month. If he missed a month, he would present her with two on the next occasion. His mother, now in her nineties, could not, of course, not be present at her only son's birthday and had even managed to climb the small hill by the sea with the assistance of Olive, her lifelong housemaid, to collect a blue orchid.

Charles managed to protect the island and to resist attempts to commercialise it by buying land from the islanders who were in need, so that having enough to live on they did not succumb to the temptation of the easy profit to be made from tourism.

The only exceptions were the taverna on the beach, which was started by Eno, a middle-aged Australian expatriate who had returned to her place of birth, having inherited the land on which she built it; and the northern mountainous part of the island which had been occupied for centuries by the monastery of St Antonios, where some fifty or so monks engaged in their daily prayers awaiting the second coming of their Master. They kept themselves isolated apart from some occasions, but for the annual celebration of their patron saint's name day, they were allowed to interact with the locals and even trade their produce, mainly wine.

Charles had promised the mayor of the only town on the island that he would not develop the land that he was buying and he kept his promise throughout the lives of both himself and the mayor. He had owned almost all of the island by the time of his death, after which Edward, with the agreement of the islanders, created the Blue Orchid Resort and Spa, a unique, ultra-luxury holiday venue designed exclusively for the super-rich and the super-famous. To keep it that way, Edward had resisted all attempts to construct an airport allowing only a modest heliport which, along with the weekly ferry boat, were the only means of access to the island.

CHAPTER TWO

The boy that was delivered by the sea

Semeli had never married. She was one of the island's few spinsters, living alone after her parent's death in the old house by the sea high on the hill, a much sought-after piece of land, also known for being the only approachable spot on the island where the blue orchids could be found.

Her father, a stubborn local shepherd, had refused to sell to *Charles the Englishman* as he called him, choosing this way to deprive his only daughter of a dowry. This, coupled with her plainness, rendered her unmarriageable. In her sixties, she made a living by cooking at the taverna operated by her cousin, Eno, and collecting the wild blue orchids for the English.

It was at dawn on a Sunday whilst collecting the few orchids on the hill overlooking the sandy beach that the high pitch sounds of the dolphins broke the morning calm. She was surprised that they had approached so near as usually they avoided the rocky part of the shoreline. She was even more surprised when she noticed a bright orange inflatable dinghy been pushed along by the dolphins. Her curiosity aroused, she took a closer look, only to notice movement within it belonging to a tiny baby wrapped in an old blanket. There was a storm about to erupt and the simmering waves started to draw the dingy back into the open sea. With no hesitation she dived into the deep blue water and, being a strong swimmer, managed to grasp it from the sea to safety. She was aware that throughout her attempts the dolphins remained near the scene circling, chirping and whistling.

She rushed the baby to her house, cleaned it, dried it and fed it fresh goats' milk, produced by her only goat which she had named Lucinda.

By noon, when she had not appeared in church, the island's priest, who was alarmed at her absence, discovered her feeding the baby boy who was strangely silent, and remained so even when being christened, the local taverna owner, Eno, being the godmother. She insisted on the baby being named Arion, angering the only priest in the island who was conducting the ceremony.

"But we cannot name it Arion, that isn't a name of any saint or martyr. The church will not allow it." The priest was adamant. Eno took him aside.

"If we do not give our children Greek names and name them Pavlos, Andreas and Marios as we now do, soon we will have no Greek names left."

"Impossible, God will strike us down with thunder," Father Pavlos replied.

Eno employed the strategy of the iron fist and the velvet glove. "Every Sunday for you and your family, free lunch, to show my appreciation."

Father Pavlos was thinking…

"Maybe, well, we could do it, but when the boy is sent to the orphanage, they may change it…"

Eno and Semeli erupted jointly in anger.

"What orphanage? I will raise the boy. I will raise it here by the sea," Semeli cried out. "The sea gave it to me only the sea can take it away, nobody else."

The priest put on his formal persona.

"I am the representative of the Church in this island. The boy needs a father and a mother. He will be sent to the Mykonos orphanage, from where he will be adopted and brought up as a true Greek and Christian. This is my last word on the matter."

A contemptuous smile formed on Eno's face. She took him aside.

"Father Pavlos, you don't seem to leave me a choice. I have, you know, been a bit productive with my camera lately. You are aware that I was a famous photographer in Australia..." She rushed upstairs and produced from an envelope a number of photographs.

"You are a handsome man, and the tourist girls are lonely looking for adventure. All you need to do is to change into civilian clothes, and you have on many occasions. Oh my God, is that you on the beach, Father? Good Lord, you are not even wearing civilian clothes and neither are the ladies, all three of them. So, shall we send the baby to the orphanage, the photographs to the bishop and the newspapers, or shall we do neither, let what happens on the island to stay on the island..."

The priest blessed the newly christened Arion and delivered the wrapped-up baby to Eno who, in turn, gave it, still silent, to Semeli a gesture symbolizing the giving the baby back to its mother, and an ecstatic Semeli gratefully accepted it. On the way out, Eno whispered to the priest, "Forget the free Sunday lunch, you are not worthy."

The priest was in no mood or position to argue.

CHAPTER THREE

Arion

Arion's christening, however holy, did nothing to contribute to either his ability to speak or to his ability to communicate in any other way with the world around him. Not for the want of trying by either Eno or Semeli, who even boarded the weekly ferry to Athens where many a specialist gave as many a prognosis on the child's condition. Eno kept trying and trying by speaking to him for hours and reading to him, to no avail. Once, when she was reading to him the story of Arion and the dolphin, she saw a small reaction in his eyes which, however, was short lived.

A long time ago there lived a young man with the same name as yours. Arion. He was handsome, not so much as you, of course, but he had a talent for music so great, that he soon became the most popular musician in the known world. He travelled to Sicily for a musical competition which he won, together with many great prizes, with which he set sail for his home on Greece. The ship's crew, however, tempted by his many prizes, decided to rob him and gave him a choice of either to be killed or jump in the sea. He chose the latter and before he jumped, he played his lyre for a while, which saved his life, as some dolphins who were swimming alongside the ship came to his rescue when he jumped into the sea and gave him a ride on their backs to Corinth, where his patron punished the sailors that robbed him when they set anchor in his city.

Arion lived a long and pleasant life, at the end of which the God Apollo placed him in the heavens in the constellation of the dolphin, from where he gazes unto our earth.

***

Neurological checks and brain scans did not produce any evidence of abnormality, but the abnormality was evidenced by reality. He could not speak, could not concentrate and could hardly communicate for anything other than very basic needs. He would fall into a long semi-conscious state that lasted for weeks, without even acknowledging Semeli, who was keeping him from starvation with difficulty.

School was, of course out, of the question. The priest did not even register him with the mainland, afraid that the authorities would penalise him for failing to report the baby's existence and arrange for it to be institutionalized. On his birth certificate he entered his surname as Mylonas, Semeli's family name, but entered unknown under name of father and name of mother. So everybody accepted the situation as they were unable to do anything about it. Semeli, Eno, the priest and the island were letting time pass them by as they went about their daily routine.

The construction of the resort brought more clients to the taverna in the winter as well as in the summer months, and both Eno and Semeli benefited from the increased income which allowed them a slightly higher standard of living. Semeli even connected her house on the hill to the electricity and bought a television.

***

Arion's birthday was decided to be the date on which he was found, the first day of April and on, his reaching twelve, there was a party for him at the restaurant. He was not, as always, aware that there was a party or of the people at the party. He hardly reacted to anyone apart from, on rare occasions, to Semeli and Eno.

It was a quiet morning and the sea was calm and inviting.

Suddenly the dolphin cries filled the air and Arion stood up. He ran to the beach, took off his clothes and dived in. Semeli's heart almost stopped until she realized that the boy was swimming as fast as the dolphins. Some even said that the boy reciprocated the dolphins' squeals, engaging in some form of communication with them.

When he returned to the shore hours afterwards, he had a large tuna fish in his hand, which he gave to Eno. He then went to the house where he sat, as always, silent for hours whilst the TV screen flicked in front of him.

There followed many a similar occasion, with daily fish caught by him to be eaten by the awaiting taverna customers. He never caught more than one fish and never ate it himself.

As he grew older it became increasingly difficult for the ageing Semeli to either control his routine or to even cut his hair or beard, so that with his tall lanky frame, dark beard and long hair, he presented a scary image as he emerged from the sea, fish in hand.

By the time he was twenty he had become a complete recluse, a wanderer on the beach, a silent phantom with no communication with reality.

The village children who had initially mocked him were now too scared to approach this strange, tall creature whose only tie to the island was Eno and

Semeli, the first to give him food and the second to accept his daily fish.

***

When the food was not on the table one day when he returned from his fish delivery, he shook and shook the dead Semeli without result and fell into his autistic trance from which Eno took him out with difficulty the next day. She dressed him with even more difficulty so that he could at least be present at the funeral. He behaved normally in the church where the whole town had gathered and he followed the funeral procession to the cemetery where, strangely and uncharacteristically, he embraced the coffin and, raising his head to the sky, he let out a long scream. He then raced away, to the surprise of all who attended, even some of the guests to Edward's birthday party who saw the funeral as a novelty event to photograph and cross out on their bucket list: 'To attend a funeral and a birthday on the same date in a Greek island'.

Arion entered the empty house his face wet, with a new experience, a tear. He took off all his clothes and climbed the hill overlooking and overhanging the beach where Semeli would pick the blue orchids. He found one and collected it, and ran to the house, where he placed the flower on Semeli's empty bed on the pillow. He then climbed the hill, ran to its edge and threw himself off it, diving down into the stormy sea. He dived straight in, refusing to swim, opening his mouth and swallowing the salty water, his breath failing him, a dizziness enveloping him, a light appearing in his mind a bright light mixing with the image of Semeli.

CHAPTER FOUR

Edward

It sometimes seemed to him when growing up that he was something of an obstacle to his parent's social life, which consisted of all different types of parties — dinner parties, charity parties, garden parties, trips abroad, from Rome to New York, even Brazil, nights at the opera from Covent Garden to Milano, eating out, dancing at Annabelle's, gambling at Aspinal's casino, racing at Ascot watching tennis at Wimbledon. An endless list which left Edward on the margin and in the care of Olive, his trusted nanny until he was old enough at the age of six to be sent to boarding school.

Edward was an unusual boy. A free spirit, as his headmaster never ceased to repeat, he took to boarding school like a duck to water. It was, perhaps, the first place where he was given the attention he craved and the stage on which he could perform and demonstrate to all, his many talents.

Charles, his tall handsome aristocratic father was an undemanding, kind person who seemed not to have ever acknowledged Edward's appearance in this world. Edward, his short and overweight only son, initially tried his best to please him but soon stopped trying, concentrating instead on pleasing Edward, an aim in which he was extremely successful. He obtained a first-class degree in history and politics at Oxford and a wife, Hira, the daughter of a leading Japanese politician who gave him twins, a boy, Albert, and a girl, Hiroko.

The Rayleigh-Miller wealth was old wealth, starting from the opium wars in China where his great-great-grandfather was a general. The opium wars were caused by the attempt by the Chinese to prohibit the opium trade, which was devastating its population. The British merchants who were supplying the opium to the Chinese users would not allow it, as they would of course lose revenue, so they started the war to force the Chinese to continue to allow its use. The family then invested in shipping and shares in the stock exchange and continued its financial ascent by acquiring a substantial property portfolio in central London.

A university graduate with a young family, Edward moved to the Mayfair family home in Hill Street, a prime London address conveniently situated a short walk from the main offices of the family company.

From the first day of his attendance at the offices, it was clear to Edward that changes were urgently required to modernize the operations of the company and drag it away from the previous century where it was stuck. Within three months he had replaced all the top management and the dated cavalier company attitudes were now a thing of the past. Profit was the only word that has meaning, profit was the aim, profit was the beginning and was the end; nothing else mattered.

Thus, armed with the profit ethos, he took the family company to new heights of success whilst remaining, together with his parents, the sole joint shareholder. Charles, his father, initially put forward some half-hearted resistance to the alteration of the family company's way of carrying on business, but then gradually withdrew and handed over the reins to Edward.

Apart from increasing the family's property holdings in London as well as in the major world capitals, he ventured into new areas such as newspaper, media and commodities. He then created a new leisure activities company which provided the whole service, from jumbo jets to fly the tourists to their destinations to the acquisition and then construction of hotels and even to the supplying of foreign exchange services, for which Edward purchased some banks.

Edward also learned to appreciate good food, wine and the company of young pretty women, for whom

Edward's wealth and power, if not his short stocky appearance, were the ultimate aphrodisiac. His marriage lasted ten years. Hira, his wife, now a famous architect left him to establish herself in New York, taking the twins with her.

There followed a string of famous girlfriends, a top singer, an Oscar winning actress and an Australian ballerina he met whilst dealing with the family property interests in Sydney. They were married within a week and divorced within a year, but not before producing offspring a lovely daughter whom they named Elizabeth.

Edward was more successful and consistent in business than in his marital ventures. Within ten years the family headed *The Times Rich List* and the list of his worth was not even remotely complete, as it did not include the various offshore wealth of the family nor the secret trusts created to keep the secret wealth secret and to avoid and evade taxation.

One day his mother called him to say that she had bad news. "We will not be able to attend Elizabeth's birthday next week, terrible news. Your father failed to wake up this morning."

Edward inherited a vast family fortune the vastness of which was known only to him.

On the failure of his third marriage and the birth of another set of twins, two girls, Edward decided that marriage was not for him, substituting instead the concept of short affairs with very pretty partners. By this time, he had learned how to enjoy his wealth to the full. Private planes, one of the biggest yachts in the world, named Lucinda after his mother, homes in every city worth having a home and, of course, the must have possession of every self-respecting billionaire — a super luxury resort in one of the most beautiful parts of the world, where the gods were born and where the gods played.

***

The hotel was made available solely for the birthday party. No bookings were accepted for seven days before or seven days after the event of the year. The guest list was decided upon months before, security and culinary needs considered, and the top performers of the world music scene invited to perform and even take part in the celebrations.

The island, in view of its remoteness and inaccessibility, lent itself to a secure environment for its guests, half of whom were on every self-respecting terrorist wanted list but, to be on the safe side, the island was hermetically closed to visitors for the two weeks.

Its aerospace was also closed and patrolled by the Greek Air Force, whilst a Greek Navy frigate patrolled the sea surrounding the island. There was also an American Naval presence. There were of course, as always, collateral purposes, deals to be made, business relationships to be established, disagreements to be settled, new conflicts to be started. Four of the most important foreign ministers in the world would be in attendance.

All of Edward's wives together with all the children would be there. In fact, Elizabeth had arrived a day earlier from Australia and had had breakfast with her step sisters, the American twins, Belinda and Francine. Having just turned twenty, they were looking forward to seeing their dad, whom they hadn't seen for over two years. In that time, they had been transformed from schoolgirls to beautiful young ladies, having inherited their good looks from their mother, apart from their fiery red hair, a characteristic of the Miller genes descended directly, if not completely legitimately, from King Henry the Eighth. They were accompanied by their mother who was, by now, unhappily married to a Hollywood film producer. His mother, of course, now in her nineties, would be present. And his current companion, Anfisa, a Russian current affairs anchor woman who, as gossip had it, was on her way out, as

Edward was seen at Loulou's night club in London on Sunday evening with the daughter of the Earl of Waverley, the accomplished horsewoman, Josephine.

The whole of the top floor of the hotel was always reserved for the family. It was labelled 'the family floor' and was not available to anyone but the family members. It occupied the whole of the top floor, all one thousand square meters of it, and it consisted of a huge master apartment and four smaller apartments. It had unparalleled sea views and two state of the art swimming pools. There were two full time chefs just for the penthouses and a full array of ancillary staff, butlers, drivers and security.

The resort itself was a completely self-sustained entity, with bakeries, organic cultivations and famous wine cellars. It would, as one critic commented, even make the Gods of Olympus jealous. There was also the staff accommodation village that was designed to also be self-sufficient, with restaurants and clubs for the more than a thousand employees, for whom social interaction with the islanders was discouraged. There was no need to alter the islanders' ethos by associating with their more liberal European counterparts.

***

Edward finished his short speech to his forty or so top management employees, which followed their lunch at the company in house restaurant. It was the eve of his sixtieth birthday and he had more or less completed his daily tasks, intending to leave early to City airport, when his secretary informed him that Dominic Robertson, a partner in one of the older firms of lawyers acting for the family, wanted to speak to him urgently. Dominic met him in his office shortly afterwards. He went straight into the reason for his visit.

"I have two documents that I have instructions to deliver to you."

"Who instructed you?"

Dominic cast a glance at the portrait of General Edward Rayleigh-Miller hanging above the office fireplace, resplendent in his uniform, who bore a striking resemblance to his great-grandson. He handed the aged file to him, on which it was written in faded ink:

To be delivered as instructed in July 2018.

There were two handwritten legal documents. The first calligraphically written document began:

*This lease is made the 13th day of July 1848 BETWEEN
General Edward Rayleigh-Miller hereinafter referred
to as the LESSOR and Sander Lee Wan hereinafter
referred to as the LESSEE. Whereas: The Lessor is the
owner of the freehold interest in the whole of the land
north of the Red River and south of the Imolip
Mountains up to the border delineated red on the map
attached hereto, as the same is more specifically
described in the plan attached hereto hereinafter
referred to as the Land, being a total of 67,000 square
miles. And Whereas the Lessor has agreed with the
Lessee to lease the said Land to the lessee on the terms
herein.*

1. *In consideration of the amount of 100,000
guineas the Lessor hereby demises the Land unto the
Lessee for a term of 170 years from the 13th day of July
1848 at the rent of two hundred guineas per annum.*

Edward skipped the rest of the document, anxious
to have a look at the map. He was amazed. It was bigger
than Wales. He was handed the next document. It was
written in similar form. It was headed:

*This is a codicil to the will of me General Edward
Rayleigh-Miller dated 14th July 1848,* and it contained
only one clause: *I devise and bequeath the reversion of*

the lease dated 13th July 1848 and made between myself and Sander Lee Wan to the first-born direct male descendant of myself such surviving descendant to be wholly of European origin. In the event that there will not be such an heir the reversion of the said lease as aforesaid shall be divided equally between the descendants of Sander Lee Wan.

"How long have you known about this?"

"It was the wish of the late General that it would be dealt with in this manner. In fact, it was my great-grandfather, Dominic Robertson, who prepared both the codicil and the lease. We are merely following in their footsteps."

"But I am not an army man," Edward said, "but you are a lawyer however just like your ancestor."

Dominic shook his head.

"The General was a businessman just like you, even better."

"What is the background of all this have you researched it? What is the value of the land?"

"The General was posted at Xanderstan to protect the opium routes which were threatened by the civil war between the northern part and the southern part. So, in his usual style, he attacked both sides and, having prevailed, occupied the state for five years, secured the opium routes and made lots of money for himself as a result. He turned native for most of those five years during which the northern Xanderstanders started an armed rebellion which he defeated. As a result, he transferred all their land to himself but then, after the second treaty of the opium wars, he agreed to lease the land to the south Xanderstans, imitating perhaps in his weird way the Hong Kong lease, which was the opposite. They say he had a number of wives and concubines and many children. That's probably the reason for the reference to wholly European origin. As to value, it is anybody's guess. You will need expert advice. Better leave you now. Happy birthday."

Edward was anxious to reach City Airport, where he had taken delivery of his sixtieth birthday present to himself, a bespoke Lear jet, a state-of-the-art private plane to replace his older model. A bottle of Cristal champagne awaited his entrance, the two air hostesses anxious to offer him champagne, and not only that, marched towards him seductively. He hardly noticed them, preoccupied with the strange message he had received on his very private mobile phone.

Only two persons had the number — Albert, his older son and Richard, his personal lawyer. In addition, the device was programmed not to accept calls or messages from anyone else. *Lose the aperitifs need to parley Rabbit.* Rabbit was the nickname of Peter Tomlinson who was at Oxford with Edward, an ingenious student who had strangely vanished after graduation, not even attending the four yearly reunions. There were many a rumour, as to his fate initially and his whereabouts which, with the passage of time, subsided and eventually he was but a face on the black and white graduation day photographs.

He dismissed the somewhat disappointed girls and walked into the jet's main conference room. The armchair was occupied and the smiling face of an aged Peter confronted Edward's surprised look.

There were five minutes of small talk.

"I know your next question... What happened to me where have I been all these years?" He smiled, cracking a joke. "I will tell you but then I will have to kill you..." And he produced a document headed Official Secrets Act.

Edward knew all about Official Secrets Act documents but could not see how it related to him. He had never had any interest in that area, although he did on some occasions, in view of his international business interests, meet and even receive advice from representatives of various secret British agencies.

"There are two documents you need to sign, the first so that I can explain my disappearance and the second to be informed of the reason for my being here."

Edward hesitantly signed the first document.

"I was recruited by the secret services from high school, as was my father and his father before him, to become a member of an organisation so secret I am not even allowed to give the name to you. To be a member of this organisation is to renounce and deny your private life and dedicate it to the service of your country. In all these years I have served both the organisation, and through it my country, faithfully. I am now the acting head of the organisation which I will refer to it as the service. Its one and only purpose is to deal in matters crucial to the protection of our country and its security, where other branches of the secret services are unable to do so. We have no limit in our powers to act in case you are wondering about how I got your number. We can get anyone and go anywhere to achieve our purposes."

Edward smiled. "And what does all this have to do with me?"

"Sign here."

Edward signed the second document.

"Are you familiar with the semi-independent state of Xanderstan?"

Edward nodded.

"It's a vast mountainous area between India and China. It's of no business interest to me, or to anyone else for that matter. It's like a mini-Afghanistan without the Taliban."

"Today is the second time the name has cropped up."

Peter motioned him to sit down and produced a copy of the aged handwritten lease document which Edward had seen earlier. He pretended to read. He looked at Peter.

"So my great-grandfather was busy during his time in China."

"It's more than that, Edward. Strictly speaking the general should not have entered into this agreement, but legally there is nothing we as a government can do about it and the Chinese government will not interfere as we have the Hong Kong lease precedent."

"The general kept it a secret, didn't he?" Edward commented.

"That he did. We only recently found out about it."

"And what's it worth, all this land?"

Peter was quiet. Edward carried on. "It has no strategic position."

Peter nodded.

"It used to be the opium route to China but no longer. It has no tourist attraction. It is in reality worthless."

Peter smiled again.

"You do know you are the sole beneficiary of the estate, don't you?"

Edward knew.

"And we also know that you being Edward Rayleigh-Miller will carry out all necessary searches in the land that you are about to inherit…"

It was Edward's turn to nod.

"And if I did, what would I find out? To save me looking." Peter replied with one word.

"Uranium!"

After a minute's silence trying to reflect on the consequences, Edward asked, "Who else knows?"

"We believe the Americans do."

"And the Russians?"

"Not yet."

"How about the Chinese?" Peter was silent for a second.

"Not sure…"

"So why all the cloak and dagger, Peter? The land will belong to me. I will sell it to the highest bidder, I am not in the nuclear weapons business."

"It's not that simple, Edward. You saw from the codicil that you are the sole surviving beneficiary and that if you do not survive the land goes to the survivors of the current lessee. That man is Sandor Lee Wan's great-grandson and one of the most powerful warlords in the area."

"But I have a son," Edward started to say, only to be interrupted by Peter.

"But not wholly European."

"Ah, but I may have another…"

"We know Edward; we know. You will be approached by a number of willing buyers."

"I thought no one knows about it."

"Well, we suspect there might have been a leak, not sure but we suspect. But definitely the lessor knows about it. I mean he knows about the expiry of the lease, not sure about the uranium. I doubt that he does but, in any event, it's of great value to him."

Edward was furious.

"Look!" Peter said. "All we want you to do for the time being is to inform us if anybody approaches you. I am only warning you as you know we were friends after all. All you need to do to contact me is to press S.A.555 on your mobile and you will be put directly to me. Our country needs that land and it is your duty to deliver it to us. When you acquire it, our government will offer you the market price and you will sell it to a company that will be a front for the British government, as we want the true owner to be secret for obvious reasons. Oh, and be careful, we are monitoring all your conversations and filming you twenty-four-seven. We have also appointed two highly trained secret service agents to guard you discreetly. By the way... Happy birthday."

Edward had been in difficult situations before and he harboured an inherent contempt for all things secret. He was happy to see Peter, sad that he was, in his opinion, wasting his life in a secret world and furious that he was being watched and powerless despite his power. But Liz and Tina, the two eager air hostesses should not be kept waiting any longer. He asked the pilot to get ready to take off and settled down for a pleasant flight, with Tina, Liz and the Cristal for company. Xandestan could wait. The pilot set course for Mykonos, from where Edward would fly to Elios by helicopter.

During the flight his plans were changed by the urgent demand from the Chinese ambassador to meet him. He had met the Chinese ambassador when he was stationed in London and had formed a good impression of him. He was certainly not a man to seek a meeting without good reason. Edward suggested a meeting on his private jet, which was agreed.

When his jet landed, the ambassador's jet was already there and the two men started their meeting hastily, disregarding the usual formalities. The ambassador was brief and to the point.

"You probably already know the reason for my visit."

Edward did and there was no point denying it.

"So your information agencies are not as ineffective as people think..." the ambassador continued. "Some events are either a curse or a blessing just like the invention of fire."

"Or gunpowder," Edward added. "Which they end up becoming depends on who is the beneficiary of the blessing and how he handles the gift. What is your opinion, ambassador? How shall I deal with the curse? Or benefit from the blessing?"

"You have the experience and the ability to make a wise decision, Mr Miller. I am not here to advise you. I am merely here to warn you. To warm you, not to threaten you, and to convey to you a message from my government and inform you of their position on this matter. My government would wish to obtain ownership of the land that you are shortly to inherit. They are willing to acquire it by paying money, awarding special trading privileges or exchanging it with either property they own abroad or with exchanging it with foreign debt. They will, in summary, do their utmost to acquire it, short of using untoward measures. But there are others who will. So be careful."

Edward knew that he was expected to give an indication of his thinking.

"I am, sir, a businessman, not a politician. And I thank you for your advice. You may inform your government that I will be reasonable in my negotiations with them."

"My friend," said the Chinaman, "This is a matter where believe me, you may be as greedy as you like, but please do not be duplicitous."

And with that he took his leave, but not before saying, "By the way, happy birthday."

It was near midnight when the helicopter landed at Elios. Anfisa had stayed awake for him but he dismissed her amorous advances citing a tiring day as an excuse.

***

Edward was at a meeting in the top floor boardroom. There was tension in the air, as negotiations involving the acquisition of the latest passenger plane by Edward's family aviation company was not progressing well, the Saudi Arabian Bin Zeini family having made a higher offer.

Edward's assistant whispered in his ear. Edward excused himself, and delegated the negotiations to his right-hand man, Nicholas Levy, a Harvard graduate. It was noon and he had promised Anfisa that he would take a break from business and devote himself exclusively to her for the afternoon. She called to him from the swimming pool when he entered the apartment, a modern-day siren, and he an Odysseus unable to resist her call dived in the clear waters.

Fresh oysters and grilled calamari with some Beluga caviar, accompanied by just a glass of chilled Cristal, followed their lovemaking.

Edward slept for a whole hour. He awoke, looked at the afternoon sky upon which the setting sun had, as always, painted a work of art, and readied himself for his afternoon swim. His two bodyguards would normally accompany him on any swim in the sea, but the security surrounding the island rendered their presence unnecessary.

Edward ran to avoid his feet been burned by the still hot sand and dived into the clear blue liquid expanse. He swam slowly and methodically as he felt a calmness overcome him and, as his thoughts raced from topic to topic, from problem to problem, from wave to wave, he felt tiredness descend upon him suddenly without warning. He thought about making the same swimming motions as previously, but his arms would not obey him. He realized that he could no longer float and he took one last look at the setting sun as life quickly begun to desert him. His body submitted to the inevitable whilst his mind resisted; too soon, too sudden, too many unfulfilled aims. It felt just like the time when sleep was about to overcome him, his childhood bedtime stories resounding, Lucinda's smile and kind eyes the last image, before darkness prevailed.

CHAPTER FIVE

Arion

The memories that flashed through his mind during his dying moments were short and simple. Semeli's face covered his memories and he even caught a glimpse of a smiling picture of a kind young woman, maybe his mother, and her deep hazel eyes. He let go of his silent world... but no, not yet, he felt the surge, he felt the dolphin raising him upwards taking him back, back to the beach, back to humanity, back to where he never wanted to be, back to his black and white shadowy world...

He started pleading with the dolphin, in the high-pitched dolphin language, *please let me be I want to leave, I wish to go...* The dolphin understood, but dolphins love life... there was hesitation. And then, as the submerged dying figure of the old man floated by, the dolphins knew that there was a solution...

CHAPTER SIX

Edward and Arion

There were two bodies on the sandy beach, as dawn approached. Consciousness began to enter his mind; the beach waves gently woke him. He remembered his death, he remembered his last breath. He saw his motionless self, spread on the sand. He heard the shouts of the searchers and the steps approaching. He stood up and ran towards the taverna.

Eno had just awakened, started the daily routine, hot coffee brewing, list of shopping, when she saw him. She wrapped a tablecloth around his naked body and ushered him into the taverna.

He became agitated when the beach filled with people, drones and helicopters hovering above, policemen, bodyguards. And the ever-present paparazzi cameras flashing and clicking.

She motioned him to be quiet. She was surprised to see that he was trying to speak to her his mouth trying in vain to form words; he had never done that before. He also saw the gathering crowd and, for a moment, she saw him trying to run towards them, a glimpse of recognition in his hitherto expressionless face. And then she witnessed the terror depicted in his expression when he faced the mirror at the taverna's entrance.

A silent scream trying to escape his lips, he stood there motionless, his gaze fixed on the apparition that faced him in the mirror. Dark long hair, dark tall body, dark beard covering the young dark face from which there stared two frightened eyes.

Eno pulled him by the hand towards the stairs leading to the upstairs room, where he slowly fell into one of his autistic trances. Edward's lifeless body was by now on its way to the mortuary, news of his death featuring on breaking news around the world, whilst all sorts of theories as to the cause of his death, from conspiracy theories, assassination, suicide, to poisoning and even a staged death, he was really still alive, his double had died, started to surface.

CHAPTER SEVEN

The Awakening

He opened his eyes about lunch time. The midday sun had entered the room together with all the noises from the taverna. He saw the clothes that Eno had placed on the only chair and his hands subconsciously felt his bearded face. He tried to stand up but almost fell down, the perspective of his surroundings confusing him. The thought dawned on him — yes, he was much taller; he had to readjust his movements. He did so slowly, hesitantly. He put on the jeans and the t-shirt, looked for shoes or sandals without success, but felt quite comfortable walking barefoot.

A thousand pictures entered his mind, a mixture of unknown and familiar experiences. His mother accepting his gifts of blue orchids, Semeli collecting them, dolphins greeting him, his twin children's faces at birth, Anfisa's naked young body passionately wrapped around him, his graduation day.

He concentrated, trying to banish the conflicting images. He built up his courage, opened the door and walked downstairs to the taverna, which was completely full of people, cameras flashing and news correspondents speaking into their satellite devices. The smell of food reminded him of his hunger.

Eno, who was busy serving, saw him first and motioned him. *Arion, get some fish we have sold everything.* He looked at her perplexed. He walked to the only available table sat down and opened the menu. Eno grabbed his ear and pulled it.

"What is wrong with you today? What sort of behaviour is this, and stop playing with that menu! She grabbed the menu from him. "Go and get some fish!"

She mouthed and motioned the *go catch a fish* hand signals to him. He tried to say something but sounds did not leave his mouth. Eno relented. After all, he had been found on the beach in a bad state and his behaviour could never be predicted. She hand signalled. *Are you hungry?*

He motioned, *yes*.

"Another first," Eno thought.

She brought him some olives, feta cheese and bread, his favourites, which he devoured, running away from the taverna as soon as he had eaten the food. His steps guided him to the empty house. He switched on the television. It was in Greek a language he could not understand, but the pictures spoke a thousand words. On all the channels they were showing parts of his life, his photographs, those of his children, his wives, his girlfriends, his yacht his plane. It was like a programme he used to watch *This Is Your Life*, where famous people were taken by surprise and presented with all of their life episodes in the presence of a TV audience of adoring friends and relatives. But in this case, it was more like a "this is your death" programme. He smiled again and thought another thought, "Rumours of my death have been greatly exaggerated," but then the realization struck him, were rumours of his death really exaggerated? Was it not the death of Edward Rayleigh-Miller that was been broadcast, pictured on the world's screens? And whose body was his? In which body was his brain hiding?"

He tried again to speak, it proved impossible. And as he agonizingly repeated his attempts, a dark cloud enveloped him. It was as though somebody had switched of the light. He was immersed in darkness, unable to think or move.

CHAPTER EIGHT

The Search

The alarm was raised by Nolan, the butler, when an hour had passed. There was an established procedure that was to be followed in which the security staff was well versed, the result of hours of training. All the eventualities had to be considered and the responses activated — kidnapping, terrorist attack, assassination and finally accident. As the world's security forces had gathered for the protection of the VIPs present, all the tools were available and a frenzy of activity ensued. The American frigate patrolling the area dispatched its drones with night vision.

It was not until dawn that the drone operator spotted the body on the beach. Or was it bodies? The faint photograph was looked at again and again as the operator was certain there was a second body but its quality was so low the information was overtaken by events. The press release from the family attributed the cause of death to "drowning caused by probable failure of the heart," the only possible cause, and one which calmed down the fears of the stock market.

The police helicopter carrying Captain Ermes Androulakakis and his team of three police officers landed at the resort and immediately embarked on their investigation. The results of the post mortem would be known soon; all evidence pointed to a heart failure but Captain Ermes did not reach the upper echelons of the Greek police force by accepting anything without investigation. Who stands to gain from the death? The classic question, but in this case one that produced umpteen suspects if it transpired that the accident theory was flawed. Revenge? Again, more suspects. Spurned lovers? At least three names featured. Political intrigues?

He commenced interviewing the last person to have seen him alive and worked his way backwards. He had his assistant, Officer Anna, present when he interviewed Anfisa, a female presence, just in case. Ermes was always careful. He couldn't pinpoint at what stage of the interview his policeman's instinct raised alarm bells. Suspicion entered the interview and hovered in the air throughout. There were no contradictions. There were no obvious lies. All was as it should be. Anna confirmed it to him. But the feeling lingered. And Captain Ermes was rarely, if ever, mistaken.

The scene where the body was found was being inspected by Anna and Ermes when Anna asked, "Does anyone live at that house? They may have seen something…"

Ermes was about to tell her off for stating the obvious, thinking that perhaps her good looks had not been exceeded by her investigative capacity but then she carried on.

"I know what the report states, about the autistic young man who lives there being cared for by his recently deceased mum but you always advised us not to overlook any detail." In fact, he had put it more bluntly. "Assumption is the mother of all fuck ups."

So they walked to the house whose door was wide open and found Eros sitting on the veranda, staring at empty space. Ermes clicked his fingers, shouted, screamed, danced, without even as much as the flicker of an eyelid from Arion. Anna then dropped her pen and bent to pick it up. Ermes noticed a fleeting reaction, a minute reaction. But what of it? They left as they came, none the wiser, but the same feeling that had caused alarm bells ringing when interviewing the girlfriend was again attempting to enter Ermes' psyche.

On their way back to the resort Ermes received the medical report on Edward's medical history and medication. For a sixty-year-old and despite his epicurean life style, he was in reasonable physical condition. There was a history of heart problems in the family, as was evidenced by Edward's high blood pressure, for which he was receiving blood pressure pills, ORIZAL 40mg, which kept his blood pressure constant at 140 over 9. Generally, there was no other medication, although the report hinted at the occasional consumption of performance enhancing pills such as Chialis or Viagra.

CHAPTER NINE

Lucinda

There had been enough deaths in her lifetime and, whilst waiting for hers, she never for one second ever imagined that she would mourn her only child, as to her Edward would always be a child, a boy she had never grown tired to idolize. It was she who had asked to see the police officer in charge and Ermes was here at her request, standing in front of her on his own, as she insisted on seeing him without others present. After the normal preliminaries she went straight to the point.

"You probably are not aware of my son's long-standing custom of sending me a wild blue orchid picked from this island on the first day of each month. He was carrying out the tradition started by his father many a year ago."

Ermes nodded.

She continued, "My son died yesterday, the last day of July."

Ermes nodded condescendingly.

"Then how do you explain this?"

She pointed to a wild blue orchid lying on the veranda.

CHAPTER TEN

The Twins

Belinda and Francine were names chosen by their mother, despite Edward's objections. He wanted names more suited to his class, such as Philippa or Hillary. Names do not determine character or upbringing, the egalitarian, feminist, American mother would reply. And she was right. Both girls were fast on their way to becoming female copies of their father, determined to build on their mostly absent father's footsteps. They obviously inherited their tall good looks from their mother, but their fiery red hair was from their father. At twenty years old, they were both looking forward to their father's birthday party, but equally excited about seeing their dad, whom they hadn't met for the past two years and who would, as they kept saying, be unable to recognize them as they had transformed into young women since he last saw them. They were accompanied by their mother who was by now unhappily married to a Hollywood superstar.

CHAPTER ELEVEN

The Transformation

Edward did not venture out from the house for three days. Eno had been either visiting him or sending him food with Elpida, her young niece, who was visiting from Australia and making some extra pocket money by waiting at the taverna. She was a nursery teacher who had also decided to find her roots.

It was the usual feta cheese, salad, olives and bread. During the three lonely days Edward had begun to adjust to his situation. The autistic trances become rarer and by the third night had gone almost completely. He had adjusted to his height by walking up and down the room, looking at the mirror and the window behind it. He was more one foot taller and at least 30 kilos lighter, not to mention the abundance of hair on his head and his face. But most of all, apart from taller, thinner and hairier, he was younger, much younger, about forty years younger. And his body was a swimmer's body, a strong athletic body, one that Edward could not have ever contemplated having, not even in his wildest dreams. His once blue eyes were now brown-hazel and his body was tanned, very tanned, as was evidenced by the small white part where his short swimming suit would normally be. And that part of him did give him some discomfort, especially when the scantily clad Elpida arrived on her daily food errands.

Edward's daily routine of interminable meetings was not missed, but however hard he tried, he was not able to deal with his speech impediment. Sounds just didn't manage to exit his mouth. He could think the word but not speak it.

For three days he had watched television in Greek, a language foreign to him. He was beginning to understand some parts, especially the advertisements. On the third day, he decided it was time to leave and to begin to cope with his situation. He had found nineteen euros in the house, all the money that his mother, as he thought of her, had, and a pair of torn jeans with matching t-shirt. There were no shoes. He searched for blades to shave and a comb for his hair, or scissors, but to no avail.

It was the morning of the fourth day when he walked into the taverna where Eno and Elpida, together with the chef, were on their daily routine of preparing for the lunch. He had decided to adopt a wait and see attitude as he didn't wish to alert anyone by unusual behaviour. The problem was that he was not aware of how his host body had behaved in the time he mentally named pre-me. Although during the three days of the two psyches coexisting there was initially some token resistance by the host persona, Edward had come to realize that his host did not really possess much of a persona, apart from the scant memories that would occasionally flash before him. There were also the trances which belonged wholly to his host. He was aware of the name Arion, and during the trances Arion was in command and he had no memory of them when reverting to reality.

Eno stopped her chores and looked at him. He replied to her gaze with his eyes. Wrong move, he immediately thought as he saw the surprise on the woman's face. He looked down to the taverna floor. Eno spoke to him in Greek whilst also hand signalling.

It was Edward's turn to be surprised. The woman actually wanted him to bring fish. But from where? Was there a fish market near? He made the hand signal for money with his thumb and index finger. Eno almost fainted. He had never ever even acknowledged any one, let alone reply to the hand signals. She took his hand and called to Elpida in English.

"Elpida, we have a situation here, Semeli's funeral may have done something to him. He has hand signalled me for money."

"Are you sure?" The young Greek Australian was more comfortable speaking in English. "Let's try again."

"I will signal for him to dive for fish."

"Let's see if he replies."

Edward decided to play their game as at some stage he would have to show some signs of communication. He signalled back. Pointing to himself and the sea, *me no today tomorrow*. More surges of surprise more signals until Edward signalled, *I am hungry* and pointed to the oven where the kleftiko was almost ready, the lamb having been roasted in the clay oven for over five hours.

Eno was in shock and her movements were now on auto-pilot. And she could not of course believe her eyes when Eros actually used a knife to cut the tender meat. He realized he had overplayed his hand so he licked the plate, made a few attempts at yelping noises and run away to his house.

The afternoon found him sitting at the cliff gazing at the sea when he heard familiar clicking. His dolphin friends were calling him. Arion took over as he recognized the whistling sound that was his name.

Without hesitation, he dived towards them, clicked back a reply and, with great ease, caught a large sea bass which he took to Eno. Eno collected it gratefully ready to give it to the chef, but Arion stood in front of her preventing access. He signalled, "Money."

Eno went to the cash desk and gave him a ten euro note. He shook his head. Edward remembered the nights when a similar fish would have cost more than two hundred. She gave him another ten which he took and ran away.

The barber shop had a monopoly in the island, it being the only one around, apart from the expensive resort salons. The ageing barber, having survived many a war and experienced great upheavals, retired to his island of birth, quietly enjoying his halcyon years. Nothing surprised him any more, and Arion entering his shop and sitting on the chair whilst signalling shave and haircut was not going to intimidate him, especially since he banged the ten Euro note right on his table. He said nothing and proceed to shave and cut, an assignment that took him the best of an hour. When he had completed his task, the wild barbarian that had entered his shop was transformed into a clean shaven, short-haired and very handsome young man. He took the ten euro note and placed it in Arion's palm, signalling no thank you. Arion put his hand on his heart, a silent thank you, and walked barefoot to the shoe shop, where he bought some sandals.

It was about the time of the afternoon walk, when locals and tourists alike paraded the main beach pedestrian area and Arion, sandals afoot, shaven and groomed, stole many an admiring glance.

Within a week, Arion was supplying Eleni with half a dozen fish a day and was earning more than one hundred and fifty euros. He was careful not to betray himself and tried to gradually reveal his newly found ability to communicate, but at the same time was in a hurry to find a way off the island. Having searched the house, he had found no evidence of any formal papers evidencing his identity, although he did find Semeli's identity card. Who was she, his mother? His grandmother? How old am I? He thought maybe twenty maybe more. There were no photographs in the house. It was as though there were no memories present. Greek is not an easy language; he picked up a few words but no more, which in a way, was good, as he didn't have to pretend he didn't understand, he genuinely did not.

Elpida gave him some hope as she spoke to him mostly in English and, to encourage her, he showed that he understood a little so she tried more and more. She also taught him hand signals, drawing on her training as a nursery teacher. She was working on her iPad a number of times and he was looking over her shoulders.

She smiled at him.

"What are you looking at? It's like a television. It has music. Do you like music?"

He pressed all the buttons at once and run away.

The next day Elpida tried to show him colours. She had downloaded a playtime Australian children's programme and motioned him to sit next to her. The music played and a red ball would roll. "Red," the voice would say.

Edward nodded to the screen and Elpida. When all the colours appeared together, he placed his finger on the red ball and nodded to the elated Elpida. There followed all the rainbow colours and Elpida was hoping to start the alphabet shortly, as Arion was trying to find an excuse to persuade Elpida to let him use her iPad. He had decided to keep a diary. He had found a pencil and paper in the house, but changed his mind after he sensed that the policeman was following his every move. It was either the policeman that had first interviewed him or his sexy assistant and who knows who else… He instead drew lines for each day that passed, although by now he was fully aware of time and space and dates.

It was his fourteenth day in his new body. There was a big national religious holiday which lasted for three days and the island would be full of tourists and passing yachts. It could be the time to make his escape. But with what papers, with what money and without knowing the language or even able to speak. He was painfully aware of the Syrian refugee problem and the terrorist problem and even more aware that the image he presented was either the latter or the former.

He decided that he would steal ID documents. He would find a tourist who resembled him and steal his passport. But how to approach them? He had to be able to work with them, maybe get a job at the taverna. He decided to expedite his learning and had, by the next day, shown Elpida that he recognized all the English letters of the alphabet. For Elpida the nursery teacher, this was a major achievement and she planted a kiss on his cheek. Arion felt the gentle lips but the reaction was from Edward, who quickly pulled her to him and kissed her on the lips. She gave in willingly for an instant but then, realizing, she pulled back and pushed him away. When he went to her for his next lesson, she was not there. She ignored him and carried on with serving in the busy taverna.

When the customers at the front table left, Arion started to collect the plates and carried them to the kitchen, to the amazement of all present. Within an hour, he had become an expert commis waiter. In fact, his general demeanour and determined manner caused some of the customers to call him for an order which, of course, he duly ignored. The female customers could not hide their admiration, a fact that did not go unnoticed by either Eno or Elpida.

On the table right on the beach, a group of six young Americans were devouring Arion's catch of the day and drinking white wine, a particular favourite of Edward's, Vivlia Hora sauvignon blanc from the north of Greece. He hadn't even thought of alcohol but, seeing the bottles on the table, he was overcome with the desire for a glass at least. The men on the table, possibly singers or actors were paying scant attention to the young girl who seemed to be becoming more and more bored. She concentrated on Arion for a while, watching the way he was clumsily clearing the tables, but then her mood completely changed at the sight of three newcomers. Arion also noticed them.

Elizabeth, Hiroko and Albert, his three children, had just arrived at the taverna. Their arrival had the same effect as switching on the kettle, on Arion's psyche. Up to now, his consciousness had not fully recognized and absorbed the situation that he was in. It was as though he was an actor in a movie, sometimes a horror movie, sometimes a black comedy. He felt more like an observer than a participant. But seeing his children in the flesh, not photographs of his children, not memories of them, but the children themselves, finally reconciled Arion with Edward and gelled the two personas together, Edward having the lion's share of the resulting personality. He hovered over the table. Elizabeth whispered to Hiroko, "Do you remember this boy? You probably don't recognize him. It's the mute boy, used to have a beard and long hair."

"Oh yes, I remember he used to come with his mother to the resort sometimes. She used to bring the blue orchids. My grandmother told me that they own the only piece of land where you will always find the orchids."

Albert intervened. "Well, well, if it's not Arion." He got up and walked towards him. "Remember me? I used to try and play with you. I even gave you my old toys. No, I guess you don't." He turned to Elizabeth. "An acute autism case," he whispered. "Lack of coordination, inability to mix with people. Even subnormal intelligence."

"He seems to be doing quite well with helping and cleaning the tables," Hiroko commented.

Albert was quite for a minute observing. "Yes!" he said, "I think you are right. Strange indeed."

Elizabeth had a few glasses of wine and was eating grilled squid when she picked up a piece of bread and dipped it in what she thought was tzatziki. Alarm bells rang in Edward's mind as it was tahini, not tzatziki, a new dip that Semeli had prepared, its ingredients, olive oil, garlic and sesame seeds. Elizabeth was deeply allergic to sesame seeds. He remembered one occasion in Egypt when she almost died from asphyxiation when she had tasted some in the salad. It was not a time to hesitate. With a quick movement, he took the tahini plate from the table and, in moving it up, he knocked the bread out of Elizabeth's hand. Semeli saw the incident and intervened apologizing.

"I am sorry, sorry. I will bring another."

"Please do please do," Elizabeth said. "I love your tzatziki."

"Oh, it's not tzatziki, but you will love the tahini more, Semeli replied, it's a new dish."

"Oh, and what does it contain?" Elizabeth asked.

"Olive oil garlic and a secret ingredient, sesame seeds, crunched sesame seeds."

"Oh my god!" cried Hiroko, Albert and Elizabeth in unison, the Egypt incident flashing in their minds."

"Oh my god, I almost died."

They looked at Edward, who was still hovering. "Thank you, thank you."

"Don't bother," said Albert. "He doesn't know where his nose is, he is out of it, lost in another world."

Albert paid the bill and put the receipt in his wallet as he always did. Albert was a stickler for detail. He would deliver the receipt to the accountant.

***

It was the next day after the incident that the chief hotel accountant, Vasilis, asked to see Albert, a very unusual request which Albert agreed to, curious to find out the reason for it. His curiosity intensified when Vasilis handed him the taverna receipt. Albert looked at him angrily as if to say, you are wasting my time.

The accountant, who had been in the family employment for decades, asked Albert, "Please look at the back".

There were three rows with numbers on them, 13 7 87 21 11, 13 7 87 21 14, 27 9 1998.

"Do you know who wrote those numbers?" Vassilis asked.

Albert was speechless.

"Have you noticed how the seven is crossed in the middle?"

Albert nodded.

"Just like your father used to write it."

"How about the numbers themselves?" Albert asked. "Do they mean anything to you?"

"No, I can't say they do. But I can investigate."

"No, no need it's probably an error, no, no need to bother. Thank you, Vasilis."

"Can I have the receipt, sir, for he accounts?"

"It's okay, don't bother, it's a negligible amount."

When Vassilis left, Albert sat down, still in shock. He poured himself a Glenmorangie whisky from his father's bar. It was his father's favourite, the eighteen-year-old bottle. No ice, his father would have murdered him if he put ice in this old malt whisky. On second thought, father is not here any more, he thought, and filled the glass with ice. His reaction was caused by fear and awe as the numbers on the back of the receipt written in pencil in a handwriting very similar to his father's, were the dates of Hiroko s birth and the time of her birth, and then his date of birth being the same and the time of his birth as he was born second. The third number was Elizabeth's birthday. He remembered what he was told in the booth after the reading of his father's will.

Each day that passed evidenced more progress in Arion's behaviour. Eno never ceased to be surprised by this gradual transformation, some of which she attributed to Elpida, but most of which she had found impossible to explain. Arion could by now, only a month after Semeli's death, write words in English and had in this way established some form of written communication in addition to the signalling that he had also made progress with. Arion had also made progress with Elpida, who could not be without him for even a single minute. Father Pavlos Papapavlou, the priest who christened Arion, decided to visit him on the anniversary of forty days after Semeli's death. It was the deceased's Memorial Day when her name would be mentioned in church, requesting God to be merciful to her. Eno, who was not known for her devotion to the church was critical.

"They make us pay to be baptized to be engaged to be married and even to be divorced. They make us pay to be buried. And as if that is not enough, they make us pay for ever after we die in order to be mentioned in church by first name only so that God will keep us in his VIP garden. And how bored must he be by hearing the same names over and over. Maybe sometimes he asks the priest- which George do you mean, the baker or the taxi driver, the fisherman or the butcher? If it's the butcher, no way, I sent him to hell last year as nobody paid for his memorial. Father Pavlos whose father and grandfather were also priests had brought his son with him more to show him around as a proud father would, his son having followed in his footsteps."

"Eno," he said, "let me introduce you to my son Father Chrysanthos".

Arion normally run away at the sight of the priest but approached the two priests slowly. He remembered being mocked and shouted at by the young Chrysanthos, who was a fat bully at the time, although he had grown to be a tall, thin, handsome young man. He even looked imposing in his black robe, priest's hat, beard and long hair with a priestly pony tail. Traditionally, when an islander or any Greek Orthodox meets a priest, he kneels slightly and kisses his hand, a gesture Eno would definitely not be involved with. But surprisingly, Arion knelt, pulled the young priest's hand as though to kiss it but instead bit it. The priest screamed in pain but then, even worse, Edward pulled him to the ground and sat on him, a situation reminiscent of similar deeds by the young bully. Eno and the old priest pulled him up and father and son walked away angrily, whilst Arion sped away, but not without having in his pocket the young priest's identification card.

For the next two weeks Arion patiently groomed both his hair and beard, having managed to acquire a priest's uniform from the shop selling disguises for carnival. His ability with hand signals had progressed enough to enable him to communicate with basic concepts and he felt ready to embark on the journey. London was the destination. He had to get to London.

The ferry left every Saturday morning and Arion, dressed as a priest, having bandaged his throat, gestured to the ticket clerk who immediately accepted the fourteen euros in cash and handed over the ferry ticket to Athens.

On the boat, Father Chrysanthos kept himself to himself and pointed at his bandaged throat to any one that tried to start a conversation. He travelled to the airport by bus, having bought a one-way ticket to London on EasyJet, arriving at Luton Airport in the early hours of the morning, passing easily through customs, the official casting only a quick glance at the identification document.

Edward arrived at Paddington with the realization that he only had five pounds left after changing his twenty euros and buying a coffee at Costa. He walked to Queensway, reaching the small mews cottage by early morning. The key was underneath the second loose brick of the garden wall; it had been there for over twenty years. It was his safe house, a place of refuge just for him, nobody else. It was where he would rest, plan, even scheme on occasions. He had purchased the house at auction and registered it in the name of a Cypriot offshore company, even using a different firm of accountants and solicitors for the transaction in order to ensure complete privacy. Offshore companies were the fashion in those days, especially for those wishing to preserve their anonymity. The shares were registered in the name of nominee shareholders, usually the employees of the firm of accountants that registered the company. Similarly, the director and secretary were the same nominees, thus anybody carrying out a company search would only find the names of the nominees. The true owner was protected by having a trust document that stated that the shares in reality belonged to the actual beneficiary whose name was left blank. Further, there was a blank share transfer form that was signed by the nominees, which the beneficiary held so that at any time the name could be inserted and the shares transferred. Having opened a bank account with Lloyds Bank and transferred funds to purchase the property, he had also paid into the account large amounts periodically, to fund the upkeep of the property. He had, through his lawyer, instructed a local management agency to manage the property. All payments were made by either standing order or by a debit card which he kept in the safe, which he now opened by using the simple code he had memorized.

The card was there and at least one thousand pounds, in twenty-pound notes. He also found the company documents in the safe. Another discovery in the safe made him pause with emotion as he gazed at the Patek Philippe watch with the inscription at the back. *To my son on his eighteenth birthday.* He could actually remember the scene when, in an unusual gesture, his father had presented it to him during his coming-of-age party at Annabel's. At the time, the society papers had commented on the rarity of the antique watch and its estimated value of over two hundred and fifty thousand pounds. Edward quickly calculated its present value to be over one million pounds if sold on the open market. An impossible scenario of course, as the watch now formed part of the deceased Edward's estate and was virtually unsaleable.

The fridge was empty.

Edward tried to change into the clothes that he had in the wardrobe, but it proved impossible; he was too tall and too thin.

He walked to the high street in his priest's black robe and entered a Levi's shop where he bought jeans, shirts jackets, socks and underwear, and carried on his shopping spree at the shoe shops, the chemists and the supermarket, but not before stepping into the local Italian restaurant and devouring most of the dishes on the menu.

He checked his balance on the card account at the cashpoint machine and was pleased. Over thirty thousand pounds. An iPhone and a sim card were his next acquisitions. He then went into the nearest Internet café and, more from habit than diligence, started to type in his code in order to gain access to his emails. He was brought back to reality by the message that access was denied. Edward was not of the internet generation; he had at least a dozen secretaries to deal with that part of his enterprises. Further, he was mistrustful of the internet and the various virus hackings and other dangers it carried, so he used it vicariously but trusted only his written notes for the most important aspects of his business, especially his bank accounts, some of which were, let's say, for his eyes only and located in tax havens with access only to the persons who carried certain numbers or other means of identification. He regretted his attempt to access his emails and quickly left the café as he knew from experience that, especially in London, there were cameras everywhere.

On his return to the house, he slept until the evening when he shaved, had a shower and headed to Mayfair, the debit card in his wallet. He had a lot to consider, many a problem to solve, a plethora of actions to enact. But first, he needed to have some fun.

He could not visit his favourite places in Mayfair as they were all private clubs where he no longer was a member, so he headed straight for the bar at Claridge's. Malcolm, the head barman, looked at him strangely when he ordered, by pointing it out, a double eighteen-year-old Glenmorangie whisky, surprised that one so young had a acquired a liking for what was an acquired taste. The barman was right. Although his senses recognized the smell and the taste, his body had never had the experience of alcohol; it was a poison to it and as such it rejected it, and he retched uncontrollably, causing the barman to shake his head. Edward paid in cash and left in a hurry.

He walked into Lancashire Court, an ancient pedestrian pebble stone yard in which there were a restaurant and a wine bar. There was an open-air section which Edward used to frequent in his younger days, especially when he needed to meet new "talent", mostly young secretaries and even young trainee lawyers or bank employees looking for adventure. He decided it was safe to have a sip of a light white wine, so he ordered a glass.

"Debbie thinks you are a mysterious man," the young blonde at the next table said to him smilingly, pointing to her similarly blonde friend. Edward motioned to his bandaged neck, and typed in his iPhone."

"Sorry, lost my voice."

"Oh, even more mystery." Debbie responded.

It was only a couple of hours later that Debbie was entering the mews house in Queensway, an anxious Edward excited and curious to find out how Arion would perform for his first time. It turned out that all three participants, Debbie, Arion and Edward, were pleased with the encounter, Arion and Debbie not able to get enough of it and Edward outperforming himself many times over. Debbie was indeed a trainee solicitor from Nottingham who was curious to find as many details as possible from Edward. *How old are you, what do you do for a living, where are you from?* She would have been shocked had Edward told her the truth, which was that he himself did not have the replies.

"Can I stay?"

Edward typed in his phone. "Not tonight, have to get up early tomorrow but will call you, I mean I will message you."

She hesitantly started to leave then said, "Will cook you breakfast tomorrow?"

"Will be here at ten," and rushed out before Edward could start writing on his iPhone screen.

He felt sleepy from the day's exertions, including the solitary glass of wine he had consumed with difficulty. He was awakened by Debbie ringing the bell and bearing eggs, bacon and beans which he devoured, but not before another session.

"I have to run to the office," Debbie said after breakfast, and left before Edward could grab her for a post breakfast session. The sixty-year-old mind inside the twenty-year-old body was pleased with the new carrier of his spirit. Edward did not wish to risk using the word soul as he was not a believer in the existence of a soul. When the body dies, the brain dies, the person that was contained in the body, the sum of all that body's experiences also died; it disappeared, dust unto dust. It was as though it had never existed. Edward, suffice it to say, was not a believer in God and his many manifestations. He was a member of the Humanist Society and contributed generously to its activities.

His current body reminded him of the Mercedes 500s coupé that he had purchased recently, his previous body of the antique Mark 2 Jaguar he purchased new in 1960s. His current body was a party that was about to commence; his older version a party almost over. He took out a blank piece of paper from the office draw and wrote upon it. "Who am I?" then, "Who am I not?"

Hunger took him out of his long period of reflection. Both questions were still unanswered. He walked to Inverness Street and knocked on the door of Galatia's Greek taverna, a very exclusive small restaurant which opened for lunch only, when the famous Galatia cooked her Greek specialty dishes. There were only eight tables and a strict face control policy, which consisted of Galatia's husband, Vassilis, looking at the potential customers and if he liked them, which was rare, entry was allowed. Edward would have been allowed in immediately of course; he was a regular and a friend of the couple. Vassilis took a look at Arion and shook his head no. Arion went prepared. He brandished his iPhone on which he wrote, "Regards from Natalia".

Natalia, a waitress at the taverna, was assisted by Edward with her visa at Vassilis' request. Edward always suspected she was more than a waitress to Vassilis, and so did Galatia, who dismissed her.

Vassilis gave him the table for two next to the bar and in a quiet conspiratorial tone asked him, "When did you last see her? Where is she? Why is she not replying to my calls? Who are you…"

Edward motioned to his bandaged neck and wrote, "Later. I am hungry. Bring me the dish of the day, a coke and extra chilli".

Vassilis fetched the traditional dips. Edward drank the coke and awaited the dish of the day, which was roast lamb with artichoke on a bed of rice. He was about to leave when he heard the very familiar voice of Phillip, his ex-roommate at Oxford, now a successful banker who was, in fact, present on the day of his birthday and the day of his death. Philip was studying the classics, majoring in Latin. He was accompanied by Alberto, his youngish Italian partner, and a third man whom Edward had not come across in his previous life.

"Fate," He thought.

He asked for a pen and paper on which he wrote in Latin, "Carpe diem" (enjoy the day), which he gave to Vassilis, who hesitantly agreed to hand it to Philip and to whisper in his ear, showing him Edward. The note was returned to Edward with a question mark on it?

Edward wrote, "C D."

A further question; a further reply. "Christian Dawkins, May Eight 9.05."

Philip was visibly shaken.

Christian Dawkins was his first and greatest love, whom he had met at Oxford and who had killed himself shortly after graduating on the eighth of May at 9.05, a suicide Philip never stopped blaming himself for. It was a secret and the last person who knew of it had died on the thirty-first of July of this year and at whose funeral he himself was present.

He turned to the sender of the note but saw an empty table on which there was a further note in very familiar handwriting.

"Meet me at our pub usual time tonight."

The pub was the Shepherd's Arms, a small pub in Shepherd's Market behind the Hilton, and the time was five o'clock. Edward had some time to kill so he spent it in an Internet café trying to find details of voice specialists who could help him speak again. He found two, one a Harley Street doctor and the other a psychologist dealing with post traumatic loss of memory and even voice loss. He made two appointments for the next morning.

He took a taxi to his home and changed into his priest's disguise to return to the pub by four. He knew how careful and conservative Phillip was and he knew that he would not come alone. His suspicion was confirmed when the two non-regulars sat at the bar followed by a young lady. He discreetly left the pub.

When nobody turned up Philip walked, as he usually did once a week, to his barbers at the Hilton where he would trim his hair and have it dyed. On leaving the hotel he would walk back to his bank, where he would spend at least one hour before walking to his house in Hertford Street. He didn't see who had put the small envelope in his inside jacket pocket. He had taken the jacket off at the pub and at the barbers. He opened the envelope. The same familiar handwriting, unmistakably the handwriting of his deceased friend, Edward, and being a banker, he knew how to recognize handwriting. The question of the handwriting at the taverna was not whether the handwriting was genuine; it certainly was, but when was it written? It could have been written at any time.

The writing on the envelope was, "Res ipsa loquitor (the facts speak for themselves). Today. To the pub with security. To have hair dye (we will dye for you) but I will never die. Meet me at Roka in Green Street in ten minutes, come alone."

Edward had changed into his Levi's jeans, shirt and jacket, and waited for ten minutes after Phillip had sat at the table.

The young boy that sat next to him simply gave him a page to read. Phillip read it. It was a summary of what had transpired until now, explaining that he couldn't speak but that he understood when spoken to. Phillip looked at him with disbelief.

"Do you really expect me to believe that you are Edward?"

Edward had already written on his iPhone. "I don't believe it myself. How can I expect you to believe? But ask me anything you want."

There followed a plethora of questions. Personal questions, girlfriends, boyfriends, university friends, car registration numbers, some regarding Edward's bank accounts, business ventures which Phillip's banks had financed… By ten that night, Philip began to be convinced. Edward gave him a list of matters he wanted to be arranged for him, the they exchanged phone numbers and parted. Edward hailed a taxi for home and Phillip decided to walk the short distance to his house situated just behind the Mayfair Hilton Hotel, a three floor Victorian residence, where Alberto awaited him. He quickly went to his office, his mood signalling to Alberto, *please do not disturb*.

He had to collect his thoughts; what had confronted him was not an everyday event and he was still not convinced that his experience was a real one. He wanted to have the comfort of a second opinion, but Edward had warned him against contacting any friends or relatives. He was right in a sense as there were suspicions of foul play; the forensic report was not as yet ready and there was the ominous coincidence that Edward had died on his birthday. Just like Christian and David. There were five of them at Oxford. Five young minds brought together by class and coincidence who had spent their prime years learning together, who then went their separate ways. There were now three of them left.

The bizarre events of the day had turned his life upside down.

He looked at Edward's list carefully and went about dealing with the instructions.

1. Deliver an unused chequebook of my personal account with your bank, with the latest statement.

2. Call Akop Aznavourian of Burlington Arcade, the watch trader, and get a value of the Patek Phillipe watch that my father gave me on my birthday. I have messaged you a photo.

3. Urgently obtain blank headed papers from the Blue Orchid Hotel. Make sure nobody notices.

4. Arrange to bring at least three blue orchids from the island.

5. Check on the background and connections of Anfisa, my girlfriend, and appoint a private investigator to watch her and report on all her movements. Also, through your banking contacts, check all her accounts for the last six months.

6. Appoint a trusted investigator to obtain the birth certificate of Arion (myself). He should contact the

taverna owner, Eno, and say he is researching an inheritance claim and needs the details.

7 . Message me when ready so that we can meet, but don't mention the meeting place. We will meet at the pub, usual time.

8 . Find out the date and place of the reading of my will.

Having walked to the bank early in the morning, he dealt with most of the requests apart from the Blue Orchid Hotel blank paper and the gift of the blue orchid, which both of which were ordered and would be received the next day. He scheduled five o'clock next day to meet Edward at the pub.

***

Edward was in Harley Street meeting the voice specialist who, after one hour's examination and X-rays, was frowning noticeably.

"In all my thirty years of practice I have not encountered anything remotely resembling your case. Apart from everything else you appear to be, in fact you are highly educated and well informed despite your disability." He turned to Arion. "We can do tests for the next ten years but I believe we will not be any wiser. It is my opinion that despite there being no physical deficiencies, the time elapsed and the psychological considerations will make it highly unlikely for your condition to be reversed. In short, you may never speak. Although, there have been cases, very rare, where a sudden shock or a traumatic experience has reversed the speech impediment."

Edward nodded. He wrote on his iPhone. "Get me the Hawkins machine."

"I can get you one that's much better."

"ASAP," Edward emphasized. "Money no object."

"One week," the doctor said.

"Three days," Edward replied. He paid in cash and left.

It was almost lunch time, so he took a taxi to Berkeley Square, getting off outside the office building housing his many companies. The sign on the entrance of the two-hundred-year-old building which led to the impressive but understated reception area simply stated, "Wesley- Miller Enterprises". He sat on the bench opposite and watched people entering and leaving, amongst them familiar faces, old and new employees. He caught a glimpse of his son, Albert, walking across the small park, followed by an entourage of associates and bodyguards. Albert, now a Harvard graduate, looked more English than Japanese and having been raised in New York should have had less of a Japanese ethos than he in reality had. His grandfather had, in fact, commented at one stage that the boy was more Japanese than the Japanese. As a result, and having joined the family business, he conflicted with Edward on many occasions and not only in the business arena. Albert was very critical of his father's life style and morals as well as his attitude towards putting profit above all else.

There had been no time for any bonding to develop. There were no family holidays, no special boys' trips. There had been no time when he and Edward had seen and felt each other as father and son. There was no animosity between the two and Edward was genuinely fond of his son and pleased with his success in life but, as he himself had had no relationship with his father, he really had no role model to be guided by in his relationship with his son.

Albert had been engaged for the past year to his childhood sweetheart, the product of another mixed marriage, Japanese-American, and was planning his wedding shortly after Edward's sixtieth birthday. On some occasions Edward would reflect on how different the two of them were, but would then consider the abyss that separated him from his own father.

He followed them to Novikov restaurant where they were met with the welcome afforded to the rich and famous. Edward had a seat at the bar and ordered, by pointing to a coke, from the young, tall, dark-haired, blue-eyed barmaid who was anxious to let him know her name.

"Hi, I am Diva, would you like lemon and ice?"

He nodded. He was, of course, not used to all this attention from people who didn't know him. Had his old short, bald, fat, former self entered the same bar, sat on the same chair and ordered the same drink, Diva would not in a million years have volunteered her name. Advances were only made to him by people who recognized him and wanted something from him. Money or fame by association.

"What's your name?"

The coke had arrived. He gestured to his throat. She nodded. She gave him a smile.

"Where are you from?" she asked.

He wrote his name on his phone, "Arion. Can't you tell by my accent?"-

She smiled and commented, "English from the humour, not the accent."

She has a brain, this girl, he thought.

"I am from Lithuania," she offered.

He had filled three pages by the time Albert and his companions had finished their lunch. As they passed him he thought of following them, but Diva's blue eyes and challenging conversation prevented him from leaving.

By early evening he had had enough Coca Cola and wrote, "See you later" to Diva and signed, "Arion, who will take you to dinner tonight after you finish work at 9 meet me opposite at Sexy Fish restaurant".

He didn't wait for an acknowledgement; he knew she would be there. He had some time to kill so he walked home through Hyde Park, stopped for a sandwich at the local café and had a small nap. Having changed to casual clothes, he took a taxi to Sexy Fish, where he was impressed at how beautiful Diva looked; she had changed her uniform to simple, tight-fitting jeans. There was a queue for seats. Edward was hungry and impatient. And he had missed great food. So he messaged Phillip. "Please book me into Loulou's, table for two under your name."

Loulou's, the most exclusive Mayfair club, had a strict member only admittance policy, but Edward knew that Phillip's bank had financed the recent refurbishment and Phillip was a good friend of the owner, so he had certain privileges.

The doorman would not have admitted them but for Edward motioning to the receptionist and handing a note saying, "I am a guest of Philip Cayford". The head receptionist, who was well known to Edward, motioned to the doorman and they were let in, under the dubious gaze of the whole of the staff at the reception. They all knew Philip's weird tastes.

Edward let Diva order the white wine, as she had studied to be a sommelier in Switzerland, although he did warn her that he could not drink more than a glass. She ordered a reasonably priced Sancerre sauvignon blanc. Edward ordered the food, seared scallops for Diva, salmon tartar for himself as appetizers, and then the house specialty of beef wellington which, however, he always had without garlic as it affected his stomach. He wrote the order on his iPhone and the waiter looked at him with surprise when he read, "no garlic, it affects my stomach".

"With respect, sir," he replied, "you look fit enough and with a stomach strong enough to eat a horse."

Edward smiled. "Maybe you are right," he wrote. "Bring on the garlic."

They didn't wait for dessert. Edward asked for the bill, but it had been taken care of by Phillip. In the taxi, Diva asked him, "Who are you? You get in the top members only restaurant, you eat, you drink, you don't pay. You know so much about wine but you don't drink it?"

He kissed her fully on the lips and she forgot she had asked the questions. They were in the house in no time. Edward wished he could scream as loud as Diva did at the height of their passion. But he couldn't.

***

Edward and Philip met at five the next day at the pub, an anxious Philip still not fully at ease. He expounded his theory on birthday deaths to Edward, who replied, "I am not dead so your theory falls."

Philip handed him the cheque book and the statement of his account. He had over two hundred thousand pounds. He signed a cheque for the total amount payable to QUW2 Co Ltd, the Cypriot offshore company which owned his current home, and he dated 30th July 2017 and handed it back to Phillip with a note to pay it in the next day.

Phillip informed him that, having spoken to Akop, the watch dealer who had initially procured the antique watch for Edward's father, who was needless to say very excited, he had a valuation of one and a half million pounds. Edward had brought the watch with him in its original box in a brown envelope. He had written on the envelope, "To my dear friend Phillip, I gift this watch as I know he will appreciate it more than me". He dated the note "24th December 2016". He handed it to Philip with written instructions. "When it's sold, transfer the proceeds to a new account that you will create in the name of a new offshore company with nominee directors and shareholders. The beneficiary will be the person named on the birth certificate that you will get for me".

The birth certificate was already with them, duly translated. The boy was named Arion, father unknown, mother unknown, date of birth 12 April 1997, surname Mylonas, which was Semeli's surname.

Holding the birth certificate Edward said, "Ask your man at the island to contact the mayor to issue an identity card for me. It's important that I have it sooner rather than later."

Phillip handed him a box containing the blue orchids and a file full of A4 headed Blue Orchid Resort paper.

"Ah... and the date of the will reading is the 12th of October at the company office building."

They parted shortly after, Phillip to walk to the bank, Edward to get a taxi home. Whilst in the taxi he had a sudden and unexplained urge to run.

When the taxi stopped at the traffic lights, he quickly gave ten pounds to the driver and ran across Park Lane to Hyde Park. He was on auto mode. It was Arion running, not Edward. He raced towards the serpentine lake throwing, off his clothes, and dived into the cold waters, to the amazement of the bystanders. He swam the length of the lake, making dolphin sounds. And then, as suddenly as it overcame him, the desire to be in water left him. He walked out of the lake, unable to understand, picked up some of his clothes and ran to his house, where he fell into a deep sleep.

When he awoke it was early morning and he was hungry. He grilled a steak with fried eggs on top, drank lots of coffee, pulled out the A4 headed paper and started to write.

CHAPTER TWELVE

The Speaking Machine

Dr Bradley Maynard was pleased with the performance of the speaking machine which his technician had delivered earlier and which was now being tested by Edward, who could not stop chatting. The technician had spent over an hour adjusting it to Arion's requirements. The computerised sound was initially intimidating, but only for a short while. Edward spoke to the technician.

"I am not and never was a technical man. I do not understand how this machine works, but I am grateful that it does. I wish to commission a bespoke machine made to measure just for me. It should be more portable and lighter, but most importantly it must sound more human. And I need it ASAP. I will pay you an initial amount of one hundred thousand pounds for such a machine. I will leave a cheque here with the good doctor for collection when the machine is delivered and it is to my satisfaction."

And at that he wrote a cheque for one hundred thousand pounds leaving the payee part blank which he placed upon the doctor's desk.

The taxi driver was initially surprised to hear the request "Queensway, please," on the strange science fiction voice, but he nevertheless complied with his young customer's wish.

CHAPTER THIRTEEN

The Lawyer

For as long as she could remember, Pamela had been in love with Edward, sometimes secretly sometimes openly. It was only during a brief spell at Oxford that her feelings were reciprocated, and even then, more physically than romantically, but the rejection that ensued dampened her feelings only on a temporary basis.

It was perhaps her obsession with him that prevented this brilliant lawyer from reaching the top of her profession, settling for a much milder and more comfortable life as sole principal in her Hampstead family practice, which she had inherited from her father.

Pamela Broadbent had taken the news of Edward's death badly and she was even now contemplating the funeral when her secretary entered her office.

"There is a young man here to see you," she said, continuing, "he is slightly unusual".

"Did you ask him the reason for his visit?"

"Yes, but he said he will only speak to you."

"His name?"

Heather had written it down "Arion Mylonas."

"Maybe Greek," she whispered, adding, "he is very dishy." Edward entered the room and took a seat and quickly explained that he was using a machine to speak. She nodded. "I have been recommended by a university friend of yours, Mr Philip Cayford. I am Arion Mylonas and I am from Elios Island.

Pamela retained her composure. "And what is the purpose of your visit?"

"I wish you to represent me on an inheritance matter."

"Mr Mylonas…"

"Call me Arion, Mr Arion."

"My firm is a divorce practice; it specializes in divorce proceedings. We do not do probate or associated matters, I'm sorry."

He smiled. "But I have read somewhere that you used to be one of the leading probate lawyers in the city, during the nineties when you worked with Seymours. I have even read about the anchor case of Re Lord Elmour, which you won against all odds."

He had now won her attention.

"You seem a bit young to know all this."

"I am not as young as you think, Mrs Pinelli." At hearing her ex-married name, Pamela was shocked. The young man had done his research.

She spoke to him with a hint of respect. "OK, I will look at the matter on which you require my assistance. If I consider that I can help, I will. On one condition. If you call me Pinelli again, I will break this vase on your head."

Pamela did not wish to be reminded of her previous life when she was the most likely to succeed new employee at the firm of Prither & Prither, the three-hundred partner firm which on many an occasion had represented the Queen and her family. She had soon grown tired of the intense pressure, but mostly of the hypocrisy of the whole situation. The straw that broke the camel's back was at a chambers party, when the senior partner in the firm, a well-known womanizer, tried his luck. The topic was porn trials on which he commented, "The only porn that I am aware of takes place in my bed. What do you think, Pamela?" he said, leering at her and touching her knee.

"With all due respect," she replied, for all to hear, "I think that you are an accomplished wanker."

She shortly thereafter left the practice to set up on her own.

Pamela called Heather.

"Prepare the conference room and ask Adriana to join us. Mr Arion, I will have my trainee solicitor join us."

The conference room of this ancient sprawling house turned into office had a homely feeling. Edward recognized Adriana, Pamela's daughter, whose christening he had attended but waited to be introduced. Pamela had had a short, troubled marriage with Ernest Pinelli, now a leading Conservative Member of Parliament, the only worthwhile result of which was Adriana, who was following in her mother's footsteps.

"Mr Arion Mylonas, this is Adriana Pinelli, my trainee solicitor. She will be taking notes."

Adriana smiled at him. He smiled back.

"As you are probably aware Mr Arion, there is a 'know your client procedure' that we have to follow, so we will need two utility bills and two ID documents."

Arion was ready for this.

"I have recently arrived from Elios Island and I am staying at a friend's house. I was robbed at Hyde Park and have lost my ID documents, but I have a copy of my birth certificate. I also have a letter from my banker, Philip Cayford, confirming my identity."

At hearing Arion's place of origin, both Pamela and Adriana were beyond shock. Eros handed the brown envelope to Pamela who started to read carefully.

CHAPTER FOURTEEN

A Visit to Mother

Having left Pamela's office, Arion walked the five minutes to Netherhall Gardens, his family home, a huge Victorian building where his mother now lived alone with her two housekeepers, Olive and Agatha. Olive was almost as old as his grandmother, but still resisted all attempts to be pensioned. Agatha was her young niece whom Edward only met on the occasions of his visits to his mother. Olive had of, course, raised him and he found it difficult to exercise self-control when he saw her face to face.

"Who is it, Olive?" his mother's familiar voice.

"It's a young man, he has a delivery, he says."

He walked into the large living room, familiar grounds. Instinctively he sat in his favourite armchair and crossed his legs, an Edward-like act. His mother broke her silence after a few minutes of looking at him and the blue orchid that he had now unwrapped.

"You are the mute boy, aren't you?"

He nodded.

"Yes, my name is Arion."

"And I can hear you speak now, how amazing. Who gave you the orchids?"

"I brought them, in case you didn't recognize me."

"But I have… But I have" Tears ran down her cheeks as she embraced him.

CHAPTER FIFTEEN

Arts Club Incident

The meeting with his mother was emotionally draining and he felt a sudden weakness as the taxi was driving him to Queensway. When the taxi arrived, the driver had to knock on the window to expunge him from a light trance in which he seemed to be immersed.

He slowly entered the lonely cottage, his old mind needing rest despite the new body in which it was being carried. Hunger overtook him. It was an Edward hunger. He needed to get back in touch with his habits; he craved foie gras, caviar with vodka, pasta with truffles. The image of the exclusive Arts Club where all his culinary desires would be met with abundance entered his mind and dictated his actions. By nine, dressed and showered, tall dark, young and very handsome, he got out of the taxi at 40 Dover Street, to be greeted by Mosey, the head doorman in his official uniform. Edward took over.

"Hello, Moses," he always called him Moses, "are we going to Ascot this year?" A reference to the time when Mosey was the family driver.

Mosey was startled by the young man's reference to matters private between him and the deceased Edward but, without showing any emotion said, "And who may you be, young sir?"

Edward landed back to reality. He knew that unless he was accompanied by a member he would not be allowed in the club. No exceptions. He walked away silently without replying, straight into the Italian restaurant next to the club.

"Table for one, please."

The half glass of red wine he drank improved his spirits and the antipasti he ate within a minute of its arrival somewhat lessened his hunger. He was waiting for his ossobuco to arrive, when the middle-aged man opposite him said something to the waiter, who brought him another glass of red wine.

"The gentleman opposite has offered you a glass of wine, sir."

The smile on the face of the well-dressed man opposite him spoke volumes and, just as he was about to refuse, an idea formed. He raised his glass. Within five minutes he was chatting to Lawrence, a city banker having an Italian meal before he met his friend next door at the Arts Club.

By ten o'clock Edward was seated at the first-floor bar at the Arts Club on old familiar grounds. The first shot of iced Beluga vodka made him dizzy again but he carried on. He ordered some more caviar. And another Beluga. And another. He walked to the disco club in the basement where he collected a number of inviting smiles, which he dismissed, having arranged a nice table by the band and ordered a bottle of Cristal Magnum. He was not aware of the time at which Edward escaped the young body and Arion took over, but take over Arion certainly did. The champagne bottle was half empty when the red-head dancing with her boyfriend, without hesitation and invitation, sat opposite him.

"Is your name Enigma?" She planted a kiss right on his mouth, to the anger of her boyfriend who moved towards him aggressively. He got ready to be punched but the young lady grabbed her boyfriend's raised hand.

"Go away, leave now."

The young man obeyed and disappeared. She kissed Arion again. He responded.

The champagne bottle was empty when she pulled him by the hand.

"Let's go!"

He followed her to the exit, Edward having entered the club and Arion exiting it. He was about to hail a taxi when she said, "My flat is here, we will walk."

The walk to the Berkeley Square apartment eased his dizziness.

Edward woke up alone in the morning, trying to understand his surroundings, trying to remember last night. He walked to the kitchen, where he faced two young red-heads having coffee.

"Good morning, enigma man."

"Let me introduce you to my sister, my twin sister Belinda."

And on the wall, a photograph of Edward Wesley Miller, proudly standing between his two daughters at their high school graduation. Both the girls smiled at him and were unable to explain the horror that was pictured in his young face. Nor could they explain the reason that he knelt down in obvious shock and shouted as loudly as he could, really shouted in his own voice, not the mechanical voice, but his own trembling voice, "Oh my God," as he ran out of the flat...

CHAPTER SIXTEEN

The Will

The top floor of the Rayleigh-Miller building overlooking Berkeley square was occupied by the five children, their three mothers and at least a dozen lawyers. Lucinda was also in attendance.

The will would, in accordance with English law become public as soon as probate was applied for but in the meantime, it was a closely guarded secret.

Prior to the reading of the will, the specialist solicitors' firm that would apply for probate should have prepared a list of the assets and liabilities included in the estate. For this reason, Pritcher & Pritcher, the lawyers' firm, had assigned three senior lawyers who, assisted by a number of chartered accountants and the company in house accountants, had prepared a draft assets and liabilities statement. That statement would be included in the formal application for probate and it had serious tax implications for inheritance tax purposes.

Edward had revised and reconsidered his will on a yearly basis, always on the third day of January, having at all times carefully considered and taken into account the advice of his lawyers and specialist tax accountants, inheritance experts in particular, as the British state took a substantial cut from any inheritance. But there were ways, always there were ways to achieve the minimum tax results.

The assets and liabilities statement could have been the accounting equivalent of *War and Peace*. The summary alone was comprised of twenty pages. The bottom line that is the total amount of the asset value was also uncertain, as the methods of valuation varied and the values kept changing. The London property portfolio, for example, had last been valued in 2012 and had increased by at least twenty percent since then. The total value of the estate was in the region of one billion pounds sterling.

Michael Pritcher, the managing partner of the long-established solicitors' practice, begun to read.

"This is the last Will and testament of me, Edward Rayleigh-Miller." There were the preliminary specific gifts. "To my loyal assistant, Nolan Bates, I leave the sum of two hundred thousand pounds free of tax and my antique Rolls-Royce Corniche, reg. no. H A N 10. To Fiona Newman, my assistant I leave the apartment at 32 Sussex Lodge Paddington, and one hundred thousand pounds free of tax."

And so it went on for the next twenty minutes, as smaller sums and cars and some flats were divided amongst the friends and employees."

Some eyebrows were raised at the specific gift of, "I leave to Oliver Everett of 10 Kings Avenue London N10 the amount of one million pounds free of tax and the freehold interest in 10 Kings Avenue aforesaid and I direct that if my death occurs before the said Oliver Everett reaches the age of eighteen the above-mentioned gifts be held on trust for him jointly by his mother Jane Everett and a partner in the firm of Pritcher and Co."

There followed some gifts to charities. Then there came the interesting part. Hiroko and Albert, the twins, now thirty-five, would inherit the shipping part of the vast financial empire, valued conservatively at about three-hundred-million-dollars. Elizabeth, now thirty, was the sole beneficiary of all the Australian assets, which included property, mines and even a cricket club and a TV company worth about fifty million dollars. The North American property holdings and shares in listed companies of over two hundred million dollars were left to the twin girls, now twenty.

The final part of the will concerned the remainder of the estate, in common terms everything else not specifically included.

"I leave the rest of my Estate not Hereby demised wherever situated to my children Francine, Belinda, Albert, Hiroko and Elizabeth Rayleigh-Miller aforesaid in equal shares absolutely". This part of the estate would be valued on a conservative estimate at more than half billion dollars. It included among others his house in London that was registered in his name and the house contents. Edward was a keen collector of paintings which included Picasso, Hockney and Freud. His antique car collections were kept in his country residence in Bury St Edmunds, a state house situated in three hundred acres complete with farm and stables. It included the airline company and the banks and the chain of hotels, the jewel in the crown being the Blue Orchid Resort. But the important part of the remainder of the estate was the parts that it did not include, the assets that were conspicuous by their absence from the list of assets.

There were no provisions for any of the ex-wives, who received mythical alimony amounts, nor for any of the girlfriends past or present, who no doubt had received value in terms of gifts. For example, the latest girlfriend had already been gifted a one-hundred-acre woodland in Surrey, complete with house and trout farm. There was no mention of any gift to his mother; it was pointless from the inheritance tax angle as it would shortly again revert to her estate and result in more tax to be paid. But sufficient arrangements and trusts had been in force earlier to ensure that none of the parties involved would ever want for anything. And, as the press had reported often and even more so currently, the known family fortune was just the tip of the iceberg, mentioning factories in China, oil wells in Venezuela, thousands of houses in Canada and shopping centres in Eastern Europe. The question was, did the will encompass all the assets, or were assets not included, passing outside the will, as they were never in the ownership of the deceased and one cannot give what is not his officially.

Rumours of offshore companies, secret trusts and Swiss accounts were spreading like wildfire. The question was put to the company's public relations spokesman as he was entering the will reading venue.

"It is rumoured there are hundreds of millions in secret bank accounts, all operated by the deceased. How do you comment?"

Lewis Day Whatley, an ex-Member of Parliament, replied smilingly, "Ask the deceased."

He was tempting fate. As the procedure was about to come to a close, the solicitor's clerk approached him and whispered in his ear. Michael addressed the meeting, "Before we close, I need to adjourn the meeting for twenty minutes."

He exited the meeting room and headed straight for the smaller conference room, where he was awaited by Pamela and her daughter, Adriana. Michael knew Pamela, who handed him an envelope. He opened the envelope and read the handwritten document carefully.

"Do we have a handwriting report?" he asked, although he knew from reading many a memo from Edward that it was his handwriting. Pamela nodded and handed him another document. Michael returned to the room sat down and spoke to the animated audience.

"There has been a development. We have what is purported to be another will. It is a holographic document, which means it's written by hand, purportedly the deceased's, and we also have an expert's handwriting report confirming the handwriting. The lady next to me, Ms Pamela Broadbent, is the solicitor appointed executor and has asked me to read the will. Now, before I continue to do so I must state that the will is to be read without admission of its validity as indeed it was the case with the previous will. All wills are, before probate is formally granted, subject to challenges and to the jurisdiction of the English courts." With that he started to read, "This is the last will and Testament of me Edward Rayleigh-Miller of 5 Hill

Street London W1. I hereby revoke all former Wills and Testamentary dispositions made by me. I appoint Arion Mylonas of Elios Island ID no 121041997 to be the executor of this my will."

He made the same specific gifts to the employees and the charities. The same specific gifts were made to the children. Albert and Hiroko were given the shipping, Elizabeth the Australian assets, and the twin girls got what they were given in the first will. So everything was the same up to the last part, the remainder of the Estate.

"I devise and bequeath all of my real and personal property not otherwise hereby demised to Arion Mylonas date of birth 12 April 1997 of Elios Island holder of Greek identification card no I21041997."

The will was dated the 31st July 2017, signed and witnessed by two witnesses, Philip Cayford and Alberto Tagnioli. And it was written on the Blue Orchid Resort headed paper.

As soon as the reading was over, the solicitor folded the papers, handed the original will to Pamela and left the room. Pamela and Adriana followed, leaving the stunned audience in the room trying to cope with what had transpired.

"Who is this Arion Mylonas?"

Albert, the coolest of the children, was on his phone speaking to his own lawyers, while different little groups started to form around the children and the mothers. Lucinda walked out unobtrusively and one could detect a little wry smile forming on her old but determined face. At the pub opposite the offices, Philip and Edward were having a drink, Philip a whisky and Edward tea.

At seeing Pamela approaching, before she was within hearing distance, Philip whispered to Edward, "You finally did it. You actually did it. You left it all to yourself."

Edward did not reply immediately but waited for Pamela to join them.

They had a sip of their drink. When Edward spoke to them, actually spoke without the assistance of the machine, they were both obviously shocked, not least from the Englishness of his spoken English.

"I will explain later," he said. "What are the reactions, Pamela?"

"Bewilderment, of course."

"They want a meeting."

"When?"

"As soon as possible."

"Who will be there?"

"Us, their lawyers and the main beneficiaries, maybe."

"Where?"

"At the company offices at ten in the morning."

***

Edward was wearing a suit and tie he had bought at Marks & Spencer's, arriving at the company offices reception at nine forty-five. He was asked to wait. The receptionist spoke on the phone. A tall middle-aged man appeared and introduced himself.

"Detective Inspector Roy Hodgkin, sir. I would like, if possible, to ask you some questions."

"Am I under arrest?"

"No, sir, just some questions."

"Unless you arrest me, I refuse to continue this conversation. And if you do, I will sue for wrongful arrest and will still refuse to reply to any questions." He took out his mobile phone. "And I am about to call my solicitor."

"No need, sir, you have made yourself quite clear." He gave him a card. "If you change your mind."

Pamela and Adriana were already in the conference room when Edward arrived. So were Albert and Hiroko, the other children choosing to send their lawyers to represent them. Edward was glad to see Hiroko, who was staring at him intently. Albert whispered something to his lawyer. He had obviously recognized him. Albert spoke, "So, you are the mute from the island the hermit of Elios. Look at you, who taught you to dress like a civilized human?"

Pamela intervened. "Any more insults, and this meeting is over. Let me introduce my client, Arion Mylonas, Mr Mylonas this is Albert Rayleigh-Miller, Hiroko Rayleigh-Miller."

Edward said nothing at first, but when he spoke, he spoke with the assistance of the speaking machine. "Hello, pleased to meet you."

The lawyer in charge spoke. "We are here to inform you that my clients have decided to contest the will. Before they do that, we are here to explore a possible," he hesitated, "settlement". Of course, anything said is without prejudice, which means," he addressed Edward, "it is as though it had never been said so that we can negotiate freely. Ms Broadbent, we are authorised to offer your client twenty-five million pounds free of tax in order to abandon his claim."

Pamela shook her head. "We are not here to be insulted. Let's go!"

"No, wait, maybe we can improve the offer, fifty million."

"Not acceptable."

"Do you have a counteroffer?"

"Yes, we do. We offer cooperation and mutual assistance. Our client has all the goodwill to cooperate fully with your clients as long as they do likewise and act in the best interests of the company and its shareholders. If there is a court dispute, the losses suffered both in the diminution in the value of the shares and the actual running of the company will be huge and of such magnitude that the company may not recover. There is enough money for everybody. But if you decide you will fight this at court then so be it. We are ready. And we will prevail as you have seen the handwriting report. It is irrefutable. And when we do win, especially in view of the extent of our inheritance, we will come after you with everything we've got, with everything the late Edward left us, so that in the end it will be as though the late Edward has left you nothing."

Throughout Pamela's speech Edward was thinking fast. He so much wanted to have a meeting with just his children to reveal himself to them, to embrace them. "It's me, your father, I am not dead." But he had decided there were too many hidden dangers, too many hidden unknowns that dictated against his wishes. And more importantly, was he, their dad, actually alive? Was it not Edward Rayleigh-Miller that died on the 31st July 2017 and was it not his dead body that his children had buried? And yet he felt so very real, so very alive. He carried on with the acting.

Detective inspector Roy Hodgkin didn't really expect Arion Mylonas, the inheritor of one of the greatest fortunes ever to be inherited, to reply to any of his questions. So he wasn't disappointed. Far from it. He had been successful in getting a full video of the meeting, which he was now screening to Captain Ermis of the Greek Police, who was accompanied by Sergeant Anna, a pretty young police officer, whom the inspector took to immediately upon greeting her and the captain at Heathrow when he had collected them the previous evening.

The autopsy had shown no suspicious circumstances and no traces of any substances whatsoever in the deceased's blood. The case was about to close and death by accident declared when Captain Ermis stopped the declaration from proceeding as he had thought of a very important factor. The deceased was on medication. He was taking Orizal pills for his blood pressure, and possibly may have consumed a few Chiallis tablets to keep him going with all the girlfriends and air hostesses. But there was no trace of any medicines in his blood. Not possible. They would not have disappeared over such a short period of time. So someone had made them disappear, together with any other substances, by a what was commonly called a mask — what athletes would normally use to hide drug taking. But it would have had to be a very effective mask to work so well. Which is what his superior told him and ordered him not to thwart the coroner.

Until he received the call from the London inspector, who wanted the background information on Arion Mylonas, a name not immediately recognizable until Anna reminded him of the young mute man they met at the house on the beach.

"You know, the one that got excited when he saw me and brandished the pistol in his pocket."

"I don't believe it. Edward Rayleigh-Miller left hundreds of millions to this person? Why? What is the connection?"

"Let's fly back to the island, get as much info as possible."

"Not possible, we are flying to London tomorrow morning."

And the Coroner's decision has been postponed. The lawyers for the family had even asked for an exhumation. Edward was buried in the family grave that Charles, Edward's father had established on a hilly part of the island and where he expressed his wish to have his final resting place; and Edward followed him.

On arriving at Heathrow and meeting the inspector, Captain Ermis was shocked to be told that on attending to inspect the tomb and arrange the exhumation, it was discovered that the body had been removed. Edward, or his body more accurately, was missing. So Arion was the prime suspect. He was present when the death occurred and he gained most from the death. The classic example, textbook stuff. But the medical reports were unequivocal. Arion was autistic, mute, uneducated, poor and lacking both the means and the ability to orchestrate such a murder. Although from what had transpired the last month, Arion proved to be cleverer than people thought and he was now speaking and arguing fluently. What had brought about the transformation? Or was there a transformation at all? Was Arion a sleeper, an enemy agent awakened by his masters to assassinate Edward?